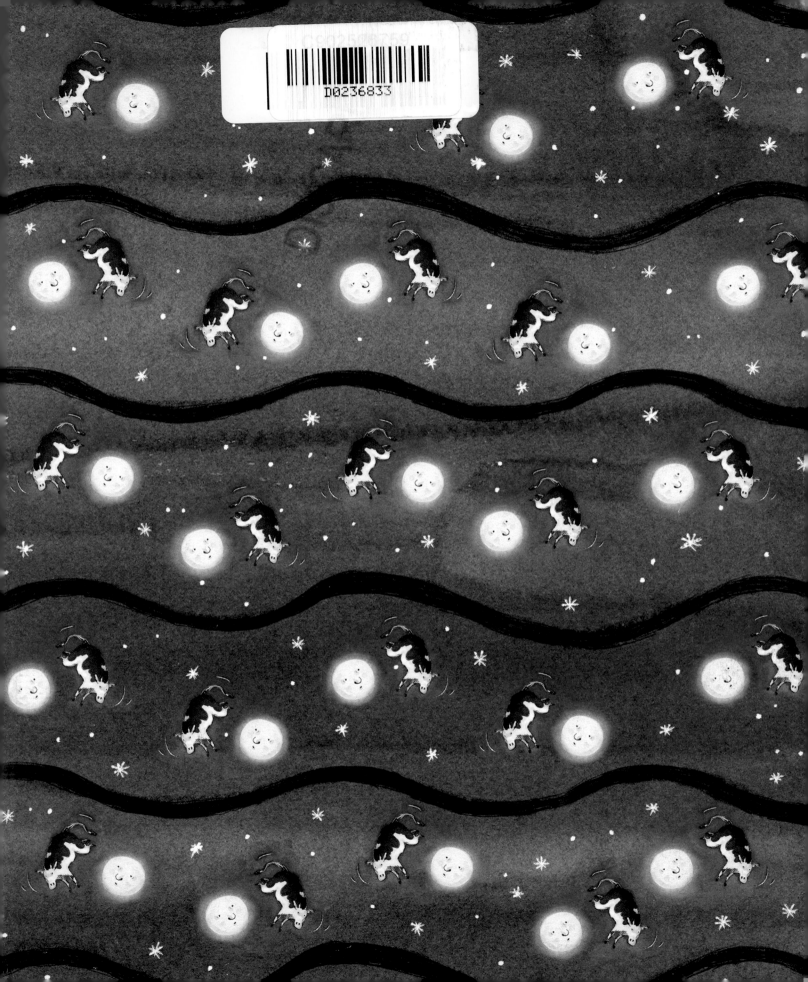

For Kenzie Tarbet Perfett, who loves cars – J.W.

For Matilda – J.S.

First published 2015 by Walker Books Ltd
87 Vauxhall Walk, London SE11 5HJ

2 4 6 8 10 9 7 5 3 1

Text © 2015 Jeanne Willis
Illustrations © 2015 Joel Stewart

The right of Jeanne Willis and Joel Stewart to be identified as author and illustrator respectively of this work
has been asserted by them in accordance with the Copyright, Designs and Patents Act 1988

This book has been typeset in Adobe Caslon

Printed in China

British Library Cataloguing in Publication Data:
a catalogue record for this book is available from the British Library

ISBN 978-1-4063-4883-5

www.walker.co.uk

THE COW TRIPPED OVER THE MOON

A Nursery Rhyme Emergency

Jeanne Willis

Illustrated by Joel Stewart

WALKER BOOKS
AND SUBSIDIARIES

LONDON · BOSTON · SYDNEY · AUCKLAND

Here comes the ambulance! It's on its way.
Who's had an accident in Storyland today?
Driver, put your foot down. Don't waste time.
This is an Emergency Nursery Rhyme!

Who have we here? It's the farmer's cow!
She fell from a great, big height somehow.
"I saw it happen," laughs a little hound.
"She tripped on the moon and fell to the ground."

She chipped a hoof and grazed her knees!
"Pass me the cow-sized plasters, please,"
says the ambulance man to the ambulance crew.
They patch her up and the cow goes "Moo!"

Here comes the ambulance! Off we go!
It's a Nursery Rhyme Emergency –
anyone we know?
Who's had an accident?
What's wrong now?

Rock-a-bye Baby fell from a bough.
The wind broke the branch
as she rocked to sleep
and Baby landed in the compost heap.

"Let's check the patient. Is she hurt?"
No, but covered in weeds and dirt,
with an old banana stuck to her head.
She just needs a bath then straight to bed.

Here comes the ambulance down the lane.
It's a Nursery Rhyme Emergency yet again!
Has Little Polly Flinders burnt her thumb?
Has Little Jack Horner choked on a plum?

Who could it be, do you suppose?

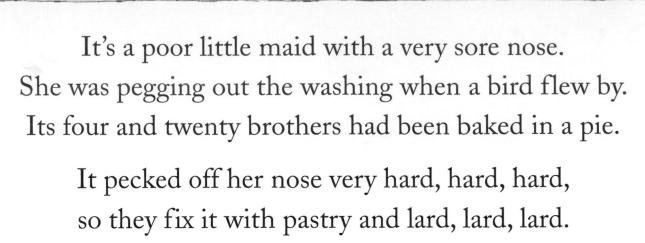

It's a poor little maid with a very sore nose.
She was pegging out the washing when a bird flew by.
Its four and twenty brothers had been baked in a pie.

It pecked off her nose very hard, hard, hard,
so they fix it with pastry and lard, lard, lard.

Here comes the ambulance! It's on another call.
It's a Nursery Rhyme Emergency! Someone had a fall.
He fell off the wall. Did he break his leg?

Who is the patient covered in egg?
All the King's Men, let the ambulance through!
All the King's Horses, shoo! Shoo! Shoo!
Humpty Dumpty has smashed his shell,
but the ambulance crew soon makes him well –
they put him together with jam and bread.
"Crumbs!" says Humpty. "They fixed my head!"

Here comes the ambulance down the hill.
It's a Nursery Rhyme Emergency – is someone ill?
Someone blew a horn but we don't know who.
Look beneath the haystack... It's Little Boy Blue!

He was meant to look after a herd of sheep,
but the poor little lamb fell fast asleep.
The cows in the corn came and nibbled the hay,
then sat on the stack where the little lad lay.
The crew checks him over: "He isn't in pain,
but he may never play on the horn again –
it's been sat on, flattened and bent out of shape."
So they fix it with hammers and trumpet tape.

Here comes the ambulance into town.
It's a Nursery Rhyme Emergency – hurry down!
The ambulance arrives and screeches to a stop.
They run to save the weasel …

but the weasel goes

POP!

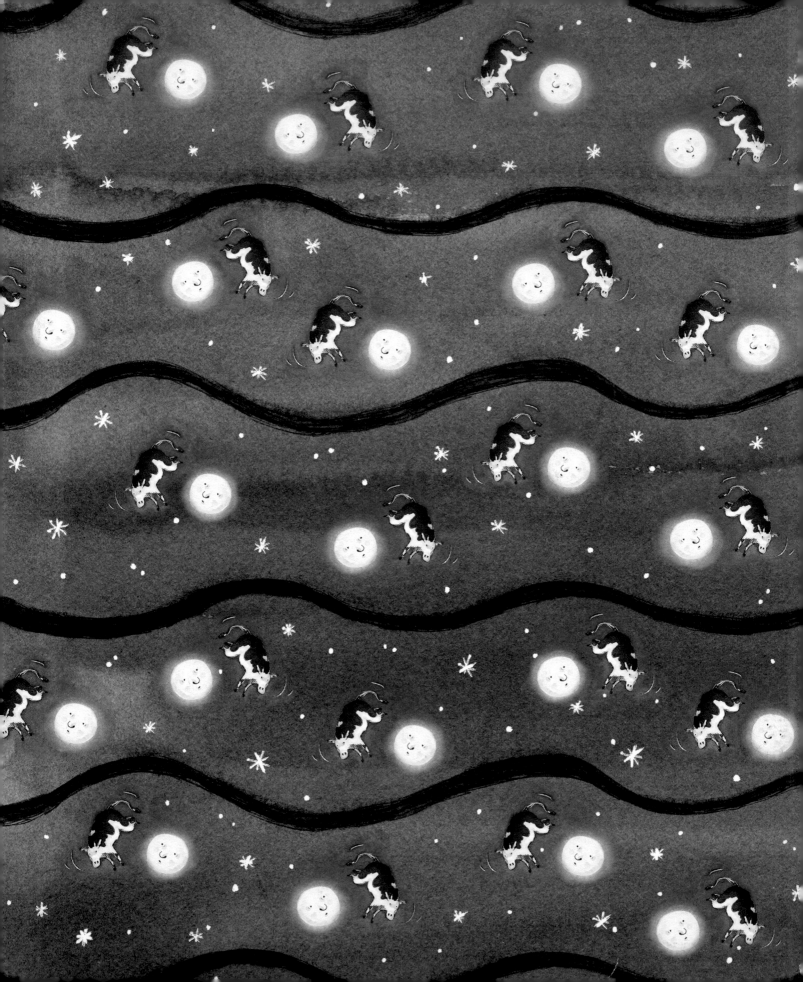